For Maria, who inspires me to dream to the moon and beyond

MR. MOON

Michael Paraskevas

CROWN BOOKS
FOR YOUNG READERS
NEW YORK

Good night, Miss Sun.

Time for Mr. Moon to awake.

The sheep should
be counted.

The clouds need fluffing.

The stars arrive, tap-dancing on a moonbeam.

The cows jump high and try to land safely.

The fireflies glitter in the trees as friendly ghosts roam, searching for a home.

Crickets croon as
the ladybugs swoon.

Mother Raccoon serves breakfast
before the school night begins.

Dewdrops prepare to greet the dawn.

The old train whistles, rumbling across the countryside toward the bright lights of the big city.

Alley cats drum a bebop beat as they rattle trash cans in the street.

"Hello, Mr. Moon," says a boy.
"Can you keep me company?
I can't fall asleep."

"Just put your head on the pillow and dream of the day ahead," says Mr. Moon.

"Dream big."

From high above, Mr. Moon keeps watch, making sure all is well.

Miss Sun pokes her head up over the hill.

"Long night," she says.
"You must be tired."

Get some sleep, Mr. Moon.

Sleep with the stars.